DISCOVERING THE DUKE

MADELINE MARTIN

OLIVER-HEBER BOOKS

CHAPTER 1

WALTON-ON-THAMES, ENGLAND,
MARCH 1814

I t wasn't the jostling carriage through the frozen country
roads that had Julia Sinclair's stomach twisting with knots;
rather it was the idea of seeing her husband again. It had been
nearly two weeks since she'd woken to find William gone after a
very awkward wedding night. He'd left a note simply stating his
need to depart at once.

On the heels of that note was yet another slip of paper found
near the hearth, crumpled as though it had been meant to join
the flames. And considering the contents, it was no wonder.
William had been called away with the insistence that he come
posthaste on account of someone called Maribel.

Maribel. The name seethed inside of Julia.

The idea of a house party in the country with her dearest
friend, the Countess of Bursbury, had been a blessing and a
curse. A blessing if William did not show, and a curse if he did.
Of course, everyone would want to see the new Duke and
Duchess of Stedton together.

Blast it.

The carriage made its way down a long drive lined with
trees, their stark limbs layered with mounds of glittering snow.

Julia pressed her temple to the cool glass window pane to better see the massive structure of Bursbury Manor in the distance. Well, that was a bit of a lie—she was actually scouring the landscape for any sign of her new husband.

Her heart rattled about her chest like a trapped bird. Dread pummeled its way into her stomach and she found herself praying that William not be in attendance. She needed these four days in the country, away from their grand home in London, away from the servants who all probably knew about her husband's mistress. Every time they gazed at her, she wondered if they were secretly pitying her, or if they were whispering gossip amongst one another.

How could she have been so stupid? This marriage was supposed to have saved her from her father's house, but now look where she'd landed herself.

Tension squeezed at the back of her throat. No. She would not crumple into tears. Not again. This whole awful mess had been given enough of her sorrow. Continuing to mourn, well, it was pathetic, and it needed to stop. And anyway, she had made her decision.

The carriage pulled to a stop before the manor, and a footman opened the door to help Julia from the small cabin. The wind hit her with a sharpness of the cold March. The chill lasted but a moment before she was swept into the grand entry of Bursbury Manor into Lady Bursbury's warm greeting.

"Your Grace." Nancy clapped her hands to her chest. "Don't you look lovely? Marriage becomes you."

"I'm still Julia to you." Julia embraced her dear friend. "Thank you for having us. Has my husband arrived?"

"Not yet, nor have I heard from him." Nancy rolled her eyes playfully. "You know how men are. I expect he'll be here any moment and without a bit of notice."

Julia gave a small laugh to keep from appearing as miserable as she felt.

Nancy waved her hand. "Come on, then. I'll show you to your chamber, so you can refresh yourself. I know the roads are just terrible. Elias told me it was a bad idea to throw a house party in March, but I thought it would be the perfect time to get out of London while it's so dismal and gray. Besides, isn't it lovely how white and sparkling the snow is out here? So much better than the grimy slush sopping the city streets."

Nancy continued to chatter on with her usual genuine excitement while she led the way, for which Julia was grateful. This felt normal, the way things were before the wedding. Before Julia realized she'd made a monumental mistake.

After having been escorted to her chambers, she took her time recovering from the journey, pausing periodically to glance out the large windows of her room. It was not the view that drew her, although it was lovely. She was on the lookout for her husband's arrival, to have the conversation she knew would not end well. Yet, it must be done.

She refused to end up like her mother.

An hour later, in a fresh gown and with her mind certain that William would not arrive in the next several minutes, Julia opened the door. There, she met a most unwelcome face. Lady Venerton, the wife of the very old, very rich earl, and a onetime friend of Julia's.

Lady Venerton did not appear at all surprised at Julia's presence. Her lips curled in a cool smile. "How wonderful to see you here, Julia." She dipped in a quick curtsey, more as an afterthought than with respectful intent.

The insult of using her Christian name was not lost on Julia.

"Lady Venerton." Julia nodded. "You look well."

And she did, dripping with gems in obscene proportions and practically glowing in a blush silk gown. It was ostentatious for daytime games at a house party, but clearly Lady Venerton had no qualms with being blatant in flashing her wealth.

"Is His Grace in attendance as well?" Lady Venerton peered around Julia, as though seeking out William.

Julia closed her door. "He is detained in the country at present and will join us if his obligations allow."

"His obligations," Lady Venerton repeated slowly. "In the country." Her lips folded in on themselves, the way one does when they have something to say, but do not wish to say it.

"Correct." Julia lifted her head and began to walk down the hall, forcing Lady Venerton to do so as well. "Is there something amiss?"

"Well, you know I don't like to gossip." Lady Venerton lowered her eyes. Most likely to hide the excited gleam there in those ice-crystal depths. For Lady Venerton loved nothing more than to gossip. Certainly, she had delighted in sharing everything she could about Julia's father.

Julia said nothing. The space of silence was all Lady Venerton needed. She clasped Julia's arm in her hot, bejeweled fingers and leaned her blonde head toward Julia's dark one. "I hate to be the one to tell you this, my darling Julia, but I have heard it on good authority that your husband has a mistress at his country estate."

Julia's stomach turned to lead and slid lower into her belly. "Oh?"

Lady Venerton pouted. "I know, and you're just newly married. But I thought you might want to know."

"Of course." It was all Julia could manage to say, especially when it wasn't anything she did not already know. And that was the worst of it, really. That the malicious words leaving those pretty lips were true.

"I've suspected for a while, to be honest," Lady Venerton continued on in the way she did, always digging the blade deeper and finding the most painful spot to twist. "After all, he often flirted with me when he was courting you. I found it inappropriate and told him I'd have nothing to do with him because he was with my closest friend, and I was quite happily married."

And by "happily married," she most likely meant "happily shopping." Still, she found her mark and twisted at that most painful spot. Heavens, the woman was skilled with wielding her wicked words.

"I see," Julia said through numb lips.

They'd made their way to the bottom of the stairs, and Lady Venerton's eyes lit up. "Oh, look! They're setting up a game of charades." And with that, she left Julia's side with the exuberance of a child, bouncing about on the energy wrought by destroying another's heart.

If Julia's mind had not been made up previously, it most certainly was now. When William arrived, Julia would tell him she wished to retire to country once she'd produced his heir. It was the only way to ease her regret at marrying him. As a woman, she had no other options.

Despite her steeled determination, she did not get the opportunity to declare her decision. Not on the first day, nor on the second. However, on the third, after a brisk walk about the frozen lake, Julia made her way into her chamber and saw the very man she wanted nothing more to do with: her husband, William Sinclair, the seventh Duke of Stedton.

And he was only partially dressed.

"Oh."

It was a simple little word, and yet it conveyed so very much to William Sinclair when it came from the wife he had spent the better part of two weeks thinking of. He'd been in the middle of dressing when the door opened, and in she had walked, stunning in her beauty.

Light spilling in from the windows turned her skin to the finest cream and shone on her glossy black hair. She'd been outside recently, as her lips and cheeks were red with the cold and her deep blue eyes sparkled like sapphires.

"Julia." He smiled at her.

She did not return the gesture. Her stare fixed on his naked chest, seeing it for the first time. He ought to put on a shirt, perhaps, but she was his wife. He wanted her to see him, to love him, to make a family with him.

A family. He wanted one of those again. The sharing, the laughter, the love. All of it. The very idea had seemed impossible for far too long.

He approached her, and she went stiff.

Confound it. He knew the wedding night had not been up to snuff, but he hadn't realized it was all that bad. But then she was so very petite, and he was so very large. He'd been terribly worried he might hurt her. Had he?

He didn't take another step in her direction. "I'm sorry I had to leave so abruptly."

"You had obligations." Her response was cool.

"I left you a note."

"I received it. Thank you."

William glanced back at his valet and found Hodges awkwardly studying a corner of the ceiling, clearly wishing to be anywhere but there at the moment.

"You may go, Hodges." William wanted the privacy as much as Hodges no doubt wanted to be free of this whole bloody conversation.

The older man said not a word. He slipped out faster than William had ever seen him move in his life, but not before shoving a shirt into William's hands as he went. The message was clear: Put on your shirt. The little push in which the garment was delivered added an insistent: Now.

William pulled on the thing before striding toward Julia. This time, she put up one small hand. "Stop."

He did as she commanded. This was most certainly not the welcome he had hoped for from his new wife. He'd anticipated nights of making up for the lost time, mending what he had botched.

"You left me on the first day of our marriage." Hurt flashed in her eyes. "And I know exactly why you left."

"There were matters of the country estate—"

"I'm well aware."

He nodded. Most likely the servants had provided his new wife with details of Maribel. They knew what her sudden illness meant to him. The horse was very dear to him, being one of the few reminders left of his father. He had been grateful to the veterinarian who had made his way to the country to see to her. His prognosis, however, was dire. And while William had missed his wife fiercely, he could not bring himself to leave Maribel's side. Not until she'd recovered.

Julia took a full inhale and drew herself fully upright, which might well bring the top of her head to the center of his chest were he standing close enough to measure. "This marriage will not work."

William's brows lifted. Surely, he had not heard correctly. "I beg your pardon?"

"Once I am in a delicate way, I wish to retire to the country." She lifted her chin and her cheeks stained with a flush. "You may live your life without the censure of a wife who will not stand by and allow you to do as you please."

What the deuce?

"I am not my mother," Julia said with finality. "I will not allow you to make a fool of me."

God, but this was uncomfortable. He was glad to not have made it in dressing yet to his cravat, lest the bloody thing feel as though it were strangling him. "Julia, the wedding night was less than ideal."

She huffed.

"You see, you are quite petite, and I am nearly twice your weight, maybe three times." He shook his head. "You were innocent, of course. I didn't——I was unsure how best to approach you." This was going so terribly awful. He ran a hand through his hair and then quickly smoothed it down. "It had been quite a while since I had," he paused under the weight of the discomfort of his admission. "You know."

"I'm afraid I do not." Julia's eyes sparked with an emotion he had never seen before. Anger?

Bloody hell.

"I do, however, know you are lying to me." She folded her arms over her chest. "It hasn't been a length of time since you've..." she went a deep red and shimmied her shoulders in a show of angry discomfort "...done *that* with a woman."

The offense of her words flashed through him. "What the devil are you on about, woman?"

"I know about the mistress at your country estate," she exploded. "I know about Maribel."

CHAPTER 2

There, it had been said.

Julia watched the expression on William's handsome face go from furrowed with irritation to wide and blank. Clearly, he was well aware he had been caught.

And then his mouth flinched at the corners. Was he *smiling*?

Julia simmered with rage. No, he wasn't just smiling. He was *laughing*.

He threw his head back and bellowed revealing every one of his perfectly white, straight teeth.

He crossed the room in two great strides of his long legs and opened his arms to her. Not that she would step into them, even if he had finally donned a shirt.

"You don't understand, my darling." His mirth faded into something gentle, and he gazed at her with the affection that had once made her heart do flips. "Maribel is my horse."

"Your...horse?" Julia asked in a small voice.

"Excuse my laughter." He stroked a hand down her cheek and a ripple of pleasure followed in its wake. "You must see the humor in your words."

She certainly felt like an absolute fool, but she gave a light chuckle nonetheless. "Forgive me. I saw a note from your steward bidding you to come to the estate for Maribel, and then Lady Venerton told me that everyone knew you had a mistress in the country."

"Lady Venerton?" He scowled. "Please tell me that odious woman is not in attendance."

A genuine laugh rose up in Julia. "I'm afraid she is."

"Had I known that, I might have found an excuse to stay longer in the country." He peered around Julia to regard the door, as if expecting the topic of their conversation to sweep in at any moment. "I'll wager she told you I flirted shamelessly with her as well, probably begged on my knees for her to be my lover. Perhaps even set up a tent below her window just to be near her?"

"I believe it was the townhouse next to hers, not a tent." Julia grinned up at her husband.

"The truth of it is she put herself in my path on countless occasions, until I finally threatened to tell Lord Venerton of her behavior. It did the trick. Nothing works like the threatening of tightened purse strings with women like that." He touched Julia's chin, tenderly tipping her face up to his. "You know the woman, and you know me."

"But I *don't* know you," Julia admitted. "Not really. We had such a fast courtship. I hadn't realized that until, well, until I thought you had a mistress, and then it struck me how little I actually know you."

"That is my fault. I wanted you from the moment I saw you. I hadn't given you enough time."

Julia's pulse quickened. "Did you?"

"I did." He gave her a lopsided smile. "Tell me what you wish to know about me, and I'll answer."

"What's your favorite color?"

"Blue."

"What's your favorite food?"

"Roasted venison."

"Do you prefer petunias or hyacinths?"

"I've always been partial to tulips myself." He remained perfectly sincere in his reply, though his twinkling eyes gave his playfulness away.

Julia forced herself to keep her face impassive. "Do you prefer being out of doors, or indoors?"

"Out of doors when it's pleasant; indoors when the weather is dastardly."

She nodded. "Fair enough."

"My turn." He ran his thumb over her lower lip. "Lips, or tongue?"

Her breath caught. *Oh my.*

Immediately, she recalled those heady kisses before the consummation of their union. When his mouth had burned like fire against her own, when the simple brush of his tongue made it seem as if the world had enveloped her in the most exquisite conflagration.

She glanced shyly down before returning her gaze to boldly lock with his. "Both."

His slow smirk indicated he clearly approved. "Shirt on, or off?"

Oh yes, *that.* Angry though she might have been when she first saw him, the strength of his broad chest, and the tight bands of muscle making wonderful ridges along his stomach, had been impossible to ignore. She had never seen a man without his shirt, though she knew well enough that such a physique as William's was not common.

"Most definitely off." She let her eyes fall closed and waited for the brush of his lips against hers.

A rap came from the door, followed by a singsong, saccharine voice. "Julia, dear, will you walk down with me to the drawing room?"

Julia sighed. "Lady Venerton."

"Julia?" William arched a brow.

Julia rolled her eyes. "We haven't been friends for ages. Not since my father—"

William released her and pulled the door open to face Lady Venerton. "Her Grace," he said with obvious stress on the title. "Is still readying herself and will be down momentarily."

"I hadn't realized you had arrived, Your Grace." Lady Venerton's tittering giggle suggested otherwise.

"Indeed," William replied dryly.

"Do send Her Grace down when you're done with her."

William said nothing more and shut the door. "That woman is vile. How did you ever consider her a friend?"

"It was a foolish mistake to let her see you in such a state of undress." Julia indicated his untucked shirt, the collar open, baring the base of his throat and the hint of his powerful chest beneath.

"She'll no longer be calling you Julia, of that you can be certain." He put his hands to her waist and carefully pulled her toward him. "And you needn't worry about me with Lady Venerton or any other woman. I don't even see any other women besides you."

He lowered his face to hers, and the flutter in Julia's stomach teased up into her heart.

A hearty knock came from the door. "Stedton, you devil, you've kept me waiting nearly three days for good company." Lord Bursbury's voice boomed from the other side of the door. "Let's get a solid match of boxing in before the ladies finish whatever it is that they do in their drawing room. Knit scarves for puppies or paint pictures of lace doilies, or something of the like."

William's head rested brow-to-brow on Julia's and he chuckled good-naturedly. "Tonight, then?"

"Tonight," she whispered. And then, as an afterthought, added. "Knitting scarves for puppies, or boxing?"

"Boxing by far, but if you see a tea cake with a lump of marzipan atop it..."

"I'll save you one," Julia promised. She placed a chaste kiss on William's cheek, and swept from the room.

Lord Bursbury offered a quick bow and had the good sense to appear uneasy at having been discovered being so very male. "Don't tell Nancy I said that when you see her."

"I'm sure she's already well aware," Julia said with a wave. "But your secret is safe with me."

With one final look back in the room at her handsome husband, she made her way downstairs for games with the ladies, anticipating the night when she would have the opportunity to discover even more about her husband.

WILLIAM BLOCKED his face and launched a fist at Bursbury's nose. The earl ducked and twisted around, exactly as William had anticipated. He delivered the final blow to Bursbury's ribs knocking the wind from him.

Bursbury bent over. "I concede."

William held out a hand to him.

Bursbury accepted and hauled himself to standing. "Three of five?" he asked jovially, unperturbed by having lost both rounds. He glanced to the garden benches where the rest of the men sat. "Any of you game for a round or two of boxing?"

Bursbury's brother-in-law, the Marquis of Hesterton, sat on a bench by himself, nursing a scotch. A neighbor of the Bursbury's, Viscount Mortry, sat in morose silence. Neither bothered to look up. Lord Venerton would certainly not be interested, as he napped with a nasal snore, his head drooping on his thin chest.

At least Venerton had bothered to come out at all. Lord Doursby had groused about the chill and kept inside.

"Hesterton?" William called out.

The marquis purposefully shifted his braced leg in answer to why he wasn't boxing. "If you wanted me to be truly miserable, you could make Lady Jane aware of my presence out here rather than force me to box." Hesterton gave an unamused smirk.

William lifted his brows to Bursbury, who answered with one of his wide grins. "Nancy's at it again with her matchmaking. Poor Hesterton has been hounded by the little debutante for the last three days." He lowered his voice. "It's really quite comical."

"I heard that," Hesterton said dryly.

"What about you, Mortry?" Bursbury regarded his sullen neighbor.

The man did not even bother to lift his dark head. "I'm already on the losing side of wrestling with my own thoughts. I don't quite think I can take on boxing." His dull gaze continued to stare off in the distance.

How very...odd. William cast a quizzical glance to Bursbury.

"Just you wait," Bursbury said quietly. "The women love him."

The French doors to the veranda opened and out poured a stream of women, resplendent in their long-sleeved outdoor attire.

"Are you boxing again?" Lady Bursbury put her hands to her hips and gave her husband a chastising look.

"It was Stedton's idea." Bursbury ran up the short flight of steps and pressed a kiss to his wife's cheek. Immediately, her stern expression melted.

"Then I hope you won." Lady Bursbury might have said something else, but Julia strode from the house at that exact moment and William's attention went immediately to his lovely new bride.

She made her way down the stairs, as he rushed toward her to keep her from having to walk on the snow in her satin slippers.

"It's freezing out here." Her breath came out in a little puff of fogged air. "I saw you boxing." She gazed up at him with wide blue eyes. "It appeared you won twice."

He cocked his head to the side in an indication it didn't matter. Truly it didn't. His accomplishments never garnered attention among the families who had fostered him.

"Impressive." Her expression turned coy. "Cards or charades?"

"Cards." He offered his hand to her to lead her back into the house. "Is it time to dress for dinner? Already?"

She accepted. "It is."

Lady Venerton swept past them, purposefully going on William's side and brushing against his person. She lingered when her breasts grazed his arm and her cheeks went pink. "Goodness, do forgive me." She blinked up at him innocently. "I was simply going to wake my husband."

William resisted the urge to wriggle his shoulder to rid it of the sensation of her touch. He said nothing and led Julia into the house.

"I told you it was a mistake to let her see you partially undressed." Julia slid him a side glance.

She was right, of course. But Lady Venerton calling her by her Christian name had raked him the wrong way. It had been a blatant insult and he would not stand for it. He only hoped Venerton would keep his wife at his side, and away from William, for the duration of the house party.

They entered the house and made their way up the stairs. A pretty young woman with light brown hair came down as he and Julia went up.

"Have you seen Lord Hesterton?" she asked.

"I believe I saw him outside a moment ago," Julia replied.

"Thank you." The woman squared her shoulders with a look of determination and practically floated down the rest of the risers.

"Lady Jane, I presume?" William queried as he led her down the hall to their shared room.

"How did you know?" Julia stopped in front of their chamber.

"I've heard there's a bit of a matchmaking going on." He opened the door and allowed Julia to enter first.

"It's Nancy. There's always a bit of matchmaking going on."

"Poor Hesterton." William shook his head, though he himself had benefited from Lady Bursbury's matchmaking with his own beautiful wife.

"Lady Jane is lovely." Julia unbuttoned her coat.

William helped her out of it and handed the heavy thing to Hodges. "It isn't that, but Hesterton has no interest in marriage."

Julia tilted her head thoughtfully. "I understand." With that, she was whisked away behind a screen by her maid.

Pity. William would have rather enjoyed watching her be disrobed in front of him, her gown peeling downward to reveal the intimate white of her chemise. Indeed, the very idea lodged in his head and his sense of hearing became intensely acute, tuned in to every whisper of fabric as it folded against itself and eventually pooled on the floor.

He settled back in his chair while Hodges lathered his face with shaving soap. It had taken a good bit of time and a considerable amount of patience on the valet's part to perfect the shave to William's preference. The process was lengthy, but the result was flawless.

"Conversation or flirting?" Julia asked from the other side of the screen.

Come out from behind that screen, dismiss the servants, and I'll show you flirting.

Hodges lifted the straight razor to allow William to reply. "A fine combination of both is enjoyable, as one without the other can be overwhelming."

A glossy swish entered the symphony of clothing being removed behind that maddening screen. He could picture it perfectly, the smooth fabric gliding over smoother skin. Hodges scraped over William's jaw, and the terrible rasp of shorn bristled hair overwhelmed the more delicate sounds.

"Blondes or brunettes?" Julia emerged from behind the screen wearing a delectable red gown.

"Brunettes." He'd have said more were it not for the razor gliding over his neck.

After a good bit of time of hair being styled, clothes being adjusted this way and that, and spritzes of expensive cologne, they were finally ready for dinner. Though he hadn't a moment to tell her how lovely she looked, not when Hesterton entered the hall a moment after them.

He glanced about furtively. "If you see—"

"Oh, Lord Hesterton, there you are!" Lady Jane was upon them in a second, her curls bobbing about her comely, glowing face.

Before the poor marquis could protest, her arm was tucked in his, and he was forced to walk her down to the drawing room. Downstairs, they discovered they were all nearly late. All, except for Lady Venerton who strode in minutes after them in an exceedingly low-cut gown, offering excuses for Lord Venerton's absence as he was apparently unwell.

That might have been well and good if it were not for the sultry gaze she leveled in William's direction, and the unfortunate fact that she was seated on his other side for the duration of a dinner that promised to be interminable.

CHAPTER 3

It was impossible for Julia not to notice Lady Venerton, and the way she fawned over William at dinner. Through five courses, the woman had chattered on with batted eyes and insipid giggles. At times, she even settled her dainty fingertips on William's forearm as she spoke. Her behavior was shameful.

Shameful and infuriating.

A sentiment that was echoed in Cecelia's gaze every time her eyes met Julia's. Lady Bursbury's niece had been a longtime friend of Julia's, and a bitter enemy of Lady Venerton.

Though William was coolly polite in his interaction with Lady Venerton, Julia could not quell the knot of unease tightening in her stomach. A hard ball of stubborn dread she couldn't dislodge.

The only thing which had brought her joy, aside from Cecelia's shared displeasure with the display, was the white puff of a dog beneath the table that readily lapped up scraps of food Julia smuggled down to it. William had tried to dissuade her against it, warning her the little beast would forever follow her around, but she hadn't bothered to listen.

In fact, with the exception of the dog, it appeared many of the guests were rather unhappy. Lord Mortry was lost in his own world of inner torment, and poor Cecelia next to him was regaled with his perpetual tales of woe. On Julia's other side, Lord Hesterton's sardonic replies to Lady Jane indicated an undeniable element of misery. There was Lord and Lady Doursly who were, well, dour — no doubt at the lackluster reception from Hesterton toward their daughter. And then there was Julia, who was lost in the storm of her own distress.

"Poor Lord Venerton," Lady Jane said, opposite Hesterton.

"Agreed," he muttered. "The poor sod has to put up with that prattling ninny for the remainder of his life."

Julia pressed a napkin to her lip to suppress a laugh.

"Oh," Lady Jane replied after a brief pause. "I was referring to his illness. I do hope he recovers quickly."

"I'm quite sure not all in attendance would agree with your hopeful sentiment," Hesterton stated with a bored drawl.

Hesterton had barely finished speaking when Lady Venerton gave a throaty chuckle at something Lord Bursbury had said.

William's hand slid over Julia's under the table. The touch should have brought comfort, but it was foreign, and the ache in her chest was far too great. She wanted to leave, to run from the room and lock herself in her chamber.

Nancy addressed the table with a pleasant expression, as if Lady Venerton hadn't flirted with every man in the room, including her husband. "Shall we leave the gentlemen to their port while we ladies retire to the drawing room? Then we can reconvene for a night of games together."

Julia almost gasped out her relief. She could finally escape with Cecelia and without the men, Lady Venerton wouldn't have the opportunity to flirt and touch William. He had been formal in return, but still polite, as was expected. Regardless, it was still too much for Julia.

She needed to get out. Now.

She rose from her chair and suddenly William was there, pulling her seat out for her. His hand caught hers. "I confess I'm grateful for the reprieve, though I'll miss your presence."

What was wrong with her? Why was this affecting her so deeply?

She nodded and tried her best to offer him a convincing smile. As soon as his back was turned, she fled and made her way to their chamber, chased there by a string of memories battering her mind. Memories of her nineteenth birthday when Mother had acquiesced to Julia's insistent begging to see the new play. However, their family box had not been empty. Father had been in the shadowed rear of it with a woman on his lap, her skirts raised as she moved over him.

He hadn't offered excuses, or even bothered to look surprised. He'd simply regarded them with an irritated scowl. They left, riding home in a painfully silent carriage. The woman had been barely older than Julia.

Even now she shuddered in revulsion.

No one had discussed it with her later. Her father had offered no apologies; her mother mentioned not one word of it. As though the entire incident had never happened. It was then Julia realized she needed to leave that house, a family that was built on lies with a father who would do...that...and a mother who allowed it.

Julia buried her horrified disgust beneath a veneer of civility, but she never forgot. Never.

Once in her room, she dismissed the servants and lay on the bed for a goodly amount of time, but the burning ache in her chest did not dissipate. Nor did the understanding she would be missed downstairs and must return.

As if on cue, a knock came from the door. "Your Grace," a gentle voice said through the door.

Julia covered her face with her hands, not wanting to see anyone.

"Julie," the woman whispered.

Cecelia.

This time, Julia rose from the mattress, drew herself together, one shattered piece at a time, and opened the door. Cecelia waited for her on the other side, a worried expression on her face. "Don't let her get the better of you."

Of course she referred to Lady Venerton.

Julie put on the bravest face she could muster. "I absolutely will not."

With that, she and Cecelia returned downstairs to attend the remainder of the night's entertainments.

However, as she was on her way to the drawing room, her husband's deep voice resonated beyond the thick wooden door where the men had congregated. "She's a beauty, with a long, thick mane of hair."

She paused, a smile softening her demeanor at the idea of her husband talking about her to the other men.

Cecelia gave a good-natured smile and waited patiently as Julia listened in on her husband's speech.

"Such a lovely creature, with a dominant personality," he continued.

A bit odd to be called a creature, but if he saw her personality as being dominant as he bragged to his peers about her, she would take it gladly.

"And she has the world in her eyes, like she knows everything." He stressed the last word. "Large and wise and the deepest shade of brown."

Julia froze. Her eyes weren't brown; they were blue. The woman her husband was discussing with such affection was not her.

Cecelia frowned, her mouth opening in question.

Julia shook her head to stop her friend. Nothing would change what they had heard. She curled her hand into a hard fist and focused on the pressure at her palm to keep from flattening herself against the door. And anyway, there was no need. Not when she could hear William's words of praise as plainly as if she were in the room with him. Certainly, she felt the impact of his subject as viscerally.

"I tell you, my girl is always ready for a bruising ride," William said.

She stiffened as Cecelia's hands flew to cover her mouth. Had he truly just said that?

"It's those gorgeous legs of hers. Long and white." He paused, presumably for a drink. "Just like her mother's."

Julia's eyes nearly bulged out of their sockets. He wasn't suggesting he'd...that, with the mother...and the daughter?

Cecelia reached for her. "Julia, come, let's—"

Julia pushed off her friend, unable to keep from listening.

"I know she's going to go soon, but it breaks my heart to see it." William sighed heavily. "I'm only glad Maribel has foaled twice, so she might forever live on in them."

Julia's shoulders dropped from where they'd climbed to her earlobes. What a blithering idiot she'd been. He was discussing his horse. Again. And she'd thought he was talking about another woman. Again.

'His horse,' she mouthed to Cecelia who chuckled silently with a shake of her head.

But Julia was not so easily given to mirth. Indeed, a sick sensation swirled in her stomach with a crushing realization. The issue was not with William at all. It was with her.

And the fear that what had happened between her mother and father could happen to her. The ache in her chest grew into something terrible. It robbed her of her breath and left her gasping for air as though she were dying.

She couldn't stand the idea of trusting William, of letting herself love her husband and then finding him the way she'd found her father. Her heart would not be able to endure such hurt. She had never realized the organ was so very fragile, yet now it hovered on the edge of shattering.

Cecelia reached for her, no doubt to guide her toward where the other women had gathered, but Julia shook her head. Her heart wasn't in it.

And how could it be with a fire burning in her chest? Cecelia did not protest as Julia returned to her room, but instead offered her a reassuring embrace of comfort. And Julia had great need of such comfort.

When he returned to their chamber, she would tell him the truth of it: she still wished to go to the country after she'd delivered him an heir.

WILLIAM TOOK the steps two at a time in his eagerness to see Julia. He'd meant to participate in the games with the rest of the house party, but when he heard she had retired to their room already, he immediately understood. She was waiting for him. To be alone with him.

He reached the landing and made his way down the hall, hoping she would still be wearing her silk frock so that he could peel it off of her. But when he opened the door, he was not met with a willing wife, but one who was red-faced from crying and wrapped in a bulky robe.

The servants had obviously been dismissed, as was evidenced by the disarray in the room. Stockings were crumpled in one corner, a pair of dainty red shoes lay on opposite sides of a chair, and various jars were left open.

"Julia, are you unwell?" He closed the door and rushed to where she sat on the edge of the bed. "Shall I summon a physician?"

She shook her head and glanced up at him. Her long lashes were spiked with moisture. "I can't do this, William. Forgive me, but I-I do not think I am meant to be a wife."

His mind reeled at her words. Were they back to this?

"I beg your pardon?" He sank to the bed beside her. "Has something happened?"

"Yes," she breathed. "I'm a coward." She buried her face in her hands, and her throat flexed as she tried with an obvious effort to hold back her tears. "I married you to escape my father's household, and now I'm realizing what I tried to leave has followed me."

How very flattering.

"I'm afraid I don't understand," William said in an even tone. It cost him dearly to keep the desperation from his voice, to keep from demanding answers. He was finally on the cusp of getting the family he wanted, but she did not want him. The same as all the families before who took him in after his parents' deaths.

The story spilled from her, of her father and his lover in the theater box. A tawdry tale to be sure.

He listened attentively. "And you think I will do this to you?"

"I worry it might someday happen." Julia gave a miserable sniff. "I hadn't realized how much I feared it, until I was reassured that you did not have a lover at your country estate. But then seeing Lady Venerton flirting with you and touching you—"

"I did not encourage her." The anger had flared up within William. The odious woman had been impossible. Toward the end of dinner, he'd had to be downright rude to keep her from putting her hands upon him.

"You did not," Julia agreed. "But someday you might. Or someday it might be a different woman whose attentions you do want." She sniffled miserably. "Then I overheard you talking downstairs about Maribel, and again, I thought you meant another woman. Do you not see, William?"

He stared at her in question. For he did not see. Not a bloody whit.

"I will forever think you are with another woman," she exclaimed. "It will drive me mad. It will drive you mad." She pressed her lips together as her eyes welled with a fresh bout of tears.

He met her gaze and put his hand gently under her chin to keep her from looking away. "I am not your father."

Her brow crumpled, and she nodded.

"Get to know me, Julia, and you will discover I am not that sort of man." He didn't bother to hide his hurt. "Get to know me and let me prove to you that you married me for more than an escape from your childhood home."

"Forgive me, William." She brushed at her wet cheeks. "Please, I need you to agree to allow me to move to the country once I've delivered an heir."

"If you still believe me to be a man who will not be loyal, and who will not love you faithfully by the time you have delivered our son, then yes, I will allow it." He chose his words carefully, intentionally.

She was correct when she said she did not know him upon their marriage. The courtship had been only two short months. Not nearly enough time to be fully acquainted. His impulsivity sometimes spun around to bite him; this was clearly one of those times. Except he would not let this opportunity slip through his fingers. He had only one wife, only one chance for a real family, and he would not lose.

Julia's shoulders sagged in evident relief. "Thank you. I am terribly sorry."

"Do not be sorry yet." He stroked a hand down her cheek. "You are still here." He pressed a tender kiss to her brow and got to his feet to prepare for bed.

He took his time unwinding his cravat, pulling off his waistcoat, and carefully folding them as he set them aside. Julia watched him with an unreadable expression. "What are you doing?"

He tugged off his shirt and squared his shoulders so every muscle in his torso flexed. She looked away, but not before giving an audible intake of breath.

"Preparing for bed." He went about the room, tidying up what had been left a disaster.

"It's early."

"Not so very early." He scooped up the discarded silk dress and carefully draped it over a chair to ensure the fabric didn't wrinkle. When he turned back to her, he found her gaze feasting on his backside before it snapped away.

His hands went to the placket of his breeches. "Are you ready?"

She gave a vigorous nod and darted under the covers, bulky robe and all. Her eyes remained averted as he unbuttoned his pants and pushed them off. She did not look at him again, not even after he'd donned his nightshirt.

He put out the candles and slid into the large bed beside her. She stiffened. He settled himself on his back and closed his eyes.

It took only a few moments before Julia began to wriggle about. A slight shifting at first, then turning and tossing about like a fish flopping on the dock.

"William?" she said finally.

"Yes?"

"Aren't you...?" she left the question hanging unsaid.

"Going to sleep?" he finished. "Why, yes, that is precisely what I'm doing. Or rather what I would be doing if you weren't squirming around."

"What I mean to say is, aren't you...going to...have relations with me?" She asked the question in barely a whisper.

And William smiled into the darkness.

CHAPTER 4

Julia's cheeks were hot with embarrassment. How awful to have had to voice such a question aloud. No wife should be forced to ask if her husband meant to have relations with her.

"No," William replied.

"Oh." She lay there awkwardly, unable to sleep and trying not to fidget. The bed had been quite a decent size the prior three nights, fluffy and comfortable and wonderfully large. Now, it appeared to be too small, every movement making her fearful she might bump or brush against him.

Well, maybe that was what she needed to do. If she was going to get with child quickly and be free of this whole marital mess, she had to be brazen enough to take action on her own.

She rolled toward him and put her fingertips to his arm. His nightshirt was thin, and the heat of his solid flesh was a welcome reprieve from the chilled night air. "William?"

"Mmmm...?"

"You're very warm," she ventured.

"You may press against me." His voice was gravelly,

suggesting he had already fallen asleep. A ridiculous notion. No one fell asleep that quickly.

She accepted his invitation and rested the length of her body against him. The simple act of putting herself against him immediately heated her icy fingers and toes. A sigh escaped her lips. He was more than warm; he was hot. And strong.

She recalled him without his shirt, the powerful cut of muscle across his broad chest. Emboldened by her goal, she trailed her fingers over his shoulder, below his neck where his skin was uncovered by the shirt, naked. His heartbeat thundered under her touch.

Still he did not react. And he was very clearly not asleep. Of that she was certain.

"Would you like to undress me?" she asked.

"We should play a game," he said abruptly.

She froze in the exploration of his body. "A game?"

"Yes." The rich timbre of his voice rumbled under her fingertips. "Tomorrow is the last day of the house party. For every game you win, you will decide what it is we do together. For every game I win, I will decide."

"That seems fair," she replied slowly into the dark. She withdrew her hand but did not turn away from the delicious heat of his large frame.

"Best of luck in the morning." With that, the infuriating man immediately fell asleep.

Julia, however, did not sleep. Not right away at least. Not with William lying beside her, hot and powerful.

A game, indeed.

She'd always been good at them and seemed to possess a considerable amount of luck. It would be simple. She merely needed to win at least once and claim her prize, which would be intercourse. She would become pregnant, deliver a boy, and be done.

It was the perfect plan.

Or so she thought.

The following morning when she awoke, William was already gone. His absence this time was welcome. After an uncomfortable night of sleeping at his side, trying desperately to keep from touching his person with any part of hers, she was all too grateful to be alone.

The door opened and her maid, Edith, entered with a silver salver. The scent of heated chocolate filled the room.

"I'd hoped you'd be awake." Edith set the tray on the small table before the fire. "His Grace ordered this from the kitchen." She straightened without bothering to restrain her grin. "He remembered that I'd requested it for you from his cook at Stedton Place. Such a thoughtful gesture."

Julia pulled herself from bed at the idea of the warm rich cup of chocolate. Her head ached, and her eyes were gritty. The treat was quite welcome to be sure. "Thank you for bringing it up, Edith."

The maid nodded and slipped from the room to give Julia time to enjoy the hot beverage. It *was* considerate of him.

And it was not his only thoughtful gesture throughout the day. He ordered a shawl brought down for her while she read in the library, even though he wasn't in there to see if she would get a chill. He complimented her on her new gown as she made her way to luncheon. In fact, it appeared he was intentionally going out of his way to bestow her with kindness.

And he most likely was.

If you still believe me to be a man who will not be loyal, and who will not love you faithfully by the time you have delivered our son, then yes, I will allow it.

His words from the night before came back to her, so carefully and purposefully stated, she knew at once what he was about. He was trying to woo her.

The idea ached to the core. If she were a different woman, one whose doubt could be as easily persuaded as her heart, it would all be so lovely. But she did not believe it possible to let go of that fear.

Wooing did not obliterate the possibility of being hurt.

One's husband, as it turned out, was impossible to avoid. William was everywhere. In their room throughout the day, passing her in the hall with a lingering smile, excelling at all masculine sports the men ventured throughout the day.

When readying for dinner, they did not talk, but he did take nearly twice as long as her to prepare. The care in his appearance was impossible not to notice, the smoothness of his sharp jawline, the immaculate combing on his hair that made one want to muss it.

Lord Venerton was in attendance at dinner, having made a full recovery. He sat beside his sullen wife, whose sparkle was relegated to her fortune of gemstones.

Without her constant interruption, William devoted his attention to Julia. And if she was being entirely honest, she was not unaffected by her husband's affection, despite her resolve to remain so. He was a handsome man, there was no denying that. It was equally as impossible to ignore those dizzying circles swirling in her stomach.

If only enjoying that sensation did not frighten her. If only the idea of loving him was not so absolutely terrifying.

So, when Lady Bursbury announced dancing would take the place of separating the sexes before games that evening, Julia knew it would be best to not dance with her husband. It was quite fortunate that he slipped away for a moment before they departed for the salon.

Cecelia was occupied by Lord Mortry, and while she looked none too pleased, nor would she be so rude as to put him off.

Julia turned toward Lord Heston. "Perhaps you would care to dance?" she asked quickly, while she had the time to do so.

The marquis paused mid-sip of his claret and set it aside to turn toward her. "With all due respect, Your Grace, it would take an act of God to get me on the dance floor."

She regretted her request even before he answered. Panic seized her, ridiculous and impossible to ward off. She was the worst kind of woman, undeserving of a man such as her husband.

Fortunately for her, Lord Hesterton cast a furtive glance toward Lady Jane on his other side, obviously having assumed Julia had asked on the younger woman's behalf.

Before William could return, Julia slipped out of the room and made her way to the library. She would return in time for the games, where she would promptly win and claim her prize. She would bear him an heir, and then settle in the country estate on her own.

For now at least, she could escape to the solitude, and recover her senses.

Or so she thought. For no sooner had the beginning notes of a lively country dance strummed to life in the salon down the hall than the door to the library swept open.

WILLIAM FOUND THE LIBRARY EMPTY, save for a fluffy white dog sitting at the base of a large set of green drapes. A large set of oddly-shaped green drapes.

"What have you got there, Bruiser?" he asked.

Lord Bursbury's dog gave a sharp yap.

"Is it an intruder that ought to be taken down?"

The shape behind the green velvet gave a little jolt. Bruiser barked again.

William crossed the room to stand by the covered windows. "Or is it a lovely duchess who has a penchant for feeding small hungry beasts, and is clearly attempting to escape the company of her husband?"

Bruiser's stubby tail waggled with such excited force, his entire body rocked side to side. Julia unfurled herself from behind the cloth, the tilt of her chin indignant.

"I was not attempting to escape your company," she declared.

William lifted a brow. "I can presume there was another logical explanation for your placement behind the draperies?"

"I was...studying the fabric. I believe we need some drapes like these in our library." She rubbed the heavy velvet between her thumb and forefinger, her lips pursed in consideration. "We most definitely do. They're quite heavy. Will you feel them?" She drew the material upright, extending it in his direction.

He did not take the fabric. "You were avoiding me."

"You are trying to woo me." She released the velvet and the panel swept back into place with a whoosh, giving Bruiser but a quick second to leap from its path.

"I am."

She crossed her arms over her chest. "You don't even bother to deny it."

"Why should I? You're my wife."

"You know why." Her cheeks flushed. "Forgive me, but I do not think I can change."

"I don't believe that for a moment."

She blinked in surprise at him.

"Otherwise why would you avoid dancing with me?" He stepped toward her, closing the distance that felt far too cold for his liking. "Why would you tuck yourself behind the draperies when you knew I'd be pursuing you?"

Her brow furrowed. "Do you expect me to answer these questions?"

"No." He gave her a half smile. "I already know the answers."

"Do you?" Her gaze drifted down to his mouth.

He lowered his face closer to hers. "I do."

"Please, elucidate me." The words were breathy with anticipation.

She thought he meant to kiss her. And he wanted to. God, how he wanted to. The prior night, sleeping beside her, knowing she was there and not touching her, it had driven him to distraction. Certainly, it had resulted in him not getting a wink of sleep. Not when he kept thinking of her slender fingertips wandering over his naked chest. He'd wanted them to wander lower, to grow bolder in exploration, more sensual.

But he needed her to want him, truly want him. He'd already broken through her shabbily erected defenses at dinner. It had been evident in the softening of her tense mouth, the genuine mirth in her quiet laughter.

He lowered his face closer still, their lips only a whisper apart. Her breath caught, and her lashes swept over her flushed cheeks.

"You're frightened," he said quietly.

Her eyes flew open. "I beg your pardon?"

"You're afraid I'll succeed in wooing you."

She leaned away from him, but he slipped his arm behind her slender back to still her from retreating.

"I know what you want, Julia."

"Of course you do." She arched her body against his, her feminine softness to his masculine hardness. "I already told you what I want."

Oh, she was sweet in his arms. Her delicate orange blossom scent teased at his resolve; her beautiful mouth parted in innocent longing. Far too tempting. He lowered his mouth to hers, stopping just before they touched.

And then he released her.

She stepped back, dazed.

"I hear games will be following the dancing." He bowed to her. "I wish you luck in our wager, my duchess."

With that, he strode from the room and left her standing beside those blasted draperies. He had only returned to the salon for a moment before Julia joined him with Bruiser trailing along behind her like a furry white shadow.

"I have it on good authority we will be playing charades this evening," she said by way of greeting. "I happen to be quite good at charades."

"And I happen to be quite good at the Petronella reel." He offered her his hand. "Would you be so kind as to join me?"

She accepted with an obvious hesitation that quickly melted away as soon as they were on the dance floor. Her sincere enjoyment of dance was one of the many things that had caught his eye about her and led to him begging an introduction from Lady Bursbury in the first place.

Following the Petronella reel was the game of charades in the drawing room. Julia was correct; she was exceptionally good at charades, her sharp wit detailing every word broken to pieces and reassembled.

Except he was better. So, when the game had drawn to a close and every participant of the house party was returning to their chamber for a final night of slumber, he found himself the victor with a prize to claim.

CHAPTER 5

Readying for bed was a never-ending task, especially when Julia was uncertain what William would request after winning. He had allowed the servants to assist them in readying for bed before he finally dismissed them. Through the entirety of it, Julia's stomach had been awash with a churning of emotions: anxiety, anticipation, excitement.

She was nearly certain his reward would not be sexual congress. Not when he was so determined to win her over. He'd been equally as determined to win at charades. He'd laughed along with the others, but when it was his turn, he had taken on an air of seriousness that spoke volumes. He'd meant to win. And he had.

She stood by the bed, uncertain if she should climb beneath the covers, or sit on the bed. In the end, she crossed her arms over the thin nightgown and waited for William to finish washing his face. Once he'd folded the towel in his immaculate way, he strode toward her in his nightshirt, one purposeful step at a time.

"You've won," she said. "What will you claim as your prize?"

He let his gaze wander down her nightgown and gave a lazy

smile that made her stomach positively twirl. "So I have. And I can ask for anything?"

Heavens! What was he planning to request from her?

"Yes," she answered cautiously.

He closed the distance between them, so her crossed arms actually pressed against his nightshirt, to the heat of his very strong chest. With gentle hands, he carefully unfolded her arms and then lifted his fingers to her face in a featherlight touch that framed her jaw. A warm tingle erupted where he caressed. His eyes were so dark in the low candlelight; she could not discern the pupil from the color surrounding it, though she knew them to be the warmest brown.

He lowered his face to hers, his sensual mouth so close, his breath brushed over her chin. Her heartbeat caught, but then thundered with undeniable impatience.

"I want to kiss you," he said in a low, intimate voice.

An eager shiver raked over her skin.

"That's all you wish for your prize?" she asked breathlessly. "A kiss?"

"Yes." His mouth lowered, and swept against hers, cool from having recently washed his face.

He did this several times, a maddening brush of their lips against one another, pausing only every now and then to kiss her bottom lip, her top lip, and then both. Fire coiled low in her belly. Her arms slid up his torso, over etched muscle and powerful strength. He was so very, very male.

His tongue touched the seam of her mouth, and she parted for him. Their tongues mated together, cautious and subtle at first, but quickly igniting with a heat echoed by the one pulsing at her core.

William's hand slid behind the back of her head, cupping it and turning her face up to him. His tongue stroked hers, his mouth kissing, nipping, sucking.

It wasn't enough for Julia. Not when he had aroused in her such a hunger. She was eager for more and more and more. The hot ache at her center was now practically unbearable.

She arched her body against his and found evidence of his own desire. A moan dragged from the depths of her soul.

He cupped her bottom with his free hand and brought their pelvises together. The hardness of his arousal met her cleft and she rubbed against him, shameless in her need, eager for that delightful friction. Their kissing went from passion to frenzy, their mouths slanting, tongues licking, breaths panting.

William held her to him and gave a low, savage growl that made every hair on her body stand on end with primal delight. With that, he broke off the kiss.

"Thank you for my prize." His chest rose and fell with his ragged breath.

Julia's mouth fell open. She watched in frustrated horror as he backed away from her and made his way around the bed.

Ravenous desire pounded between her legs, unsatisfied. A soft whimper escaped her lips before she could stop it. Every bit of her was wild with feeling, so that even the scant weight of her nightgown against her stiffened nipples made little ripples of gooseflesh dance over her skin.

She climbed into bed beside him, the sheets cool against her burning skin. What had he done to her?

She curled a naked leg over his. "William, please?"

"Please what, madam?" he asked in a low, gravelly voice.

"Please kiss me again. Touch me. Take me." She ran her hands over the swell of his chest and practically melted at the impossible strength there. "Please," she whispered.

He did not answer, and she nearly cried out. Surely, he was not asleep already. Who could possibly sleep with everything throbbing and glowing with the heat of a thousand glowing embers?

But she knew all the begging in the world would not get her what she wanted. Only winning a blasted game would, and since this was the last night, she hoped Nancy had something planned tomorrow before their departure. She needed more time.

~

THE WIND HOWLED through the night and well beyond morning. William had been awake for all of it. Judging by the rustling about and perpetual tossing and turning, so too had Julia.

He had known simply kissing her would be the sweetest torture, but he had not anticipated the level of discomfort his unsatisfied body would heap upon him. His groin ached, and his veins seemed to pulse with thick mud rather than blood.

It was the first time in the fortnight of their marriage he'd woken up with his wife. Dark hair tousled around her face, making her look pleasantly mussed, as though she'd been well-loved rather than having slept poorly.

Her mouth curled into a shy smile. "Good morning."

Her nightgown had slipped from one shoulder, leaving it bare and tempting in the light easing in from around the edge of the curtains. She followed his gaze and quickly pushed up the drooping cloth. That wasn't all. She grasped the covers and tucked them about under her arms with the yards of thick cloth layered over her like a shield.

He raised his brows. "For a woman who wishes me to move along in the business of procreation, you certainly are rather missish this morning."

"But the sun is up."

Oh yes, the sun was up. And that was how he'd prefer to see her best, with those golden rays kissing her flawless skin. "Once

I have finally had you again, wife, I will have you anywhere and at any hour."

She stammered, "I beg your pardon?"

"Including in the full light of day." He tugged lightly at the blanket. It fell free from her limp grasp to reveal one soft pink nipple beneath the thin linen nightgown. "Where I can see all of you. Touch all of you." He grinned as the little bud grew taut and strained at the fabric. "Taste all of you."

Her mouth parted, but before she could say more, he drew away, more for his sake than for her own. God, he ached fiercely for her. Acutely.

To his surprise, she slipped from the bed as well, and did not bother to put on her robe. Sunlight limned the outline of her body beneath, highlighting the dip of her waist and an enticing line of light between her slender thighs. He pulled back a corner of the curtain in desperate need to escape and was blinded with the brilliance of sheer white outside.

Julia drew back with him, shielding her eyes. Together, they blinked and gazed out once more. A thick layer of snow coated the world beyond, hiding the exact location of the lake and burying bushes. The roads would be impassable for travel regardless.

"I think we will be staying here for another day," Julia said brightly.

"At least. Why does that have you so happy?"

"It's another day to win games." She smiled. "It's my turn." Her gaze fell on his forearm where his nightshirt had ridden up and her quiet joy faltered. "What happened there?"

William brushed the sleeve into place, covering the mottled flesh. He'd made sure to keep that arm turned from Julia's sight until now. It ran along the outside of his forearm, a violent mass of thick, twisted skin. A small scar by comparison to what it could have been, how close he'd come to death.

"A burn, that is all." He released the drapes and the room blanketed in darkness.

"Were you in a fire?" she asked.

"Yes." He strode away from the windows and went to the ewer to wash his face.

"When?"

Why did she have to press him so? He splashed cold water on his face, but it did not blot out the memories of that day, the screams of his parents as the flames consumed them. He scrubbed at his face, but he could not scour away the weight of guilt in his heart. A lifetime of consideration had taught him that it would never lessen. He folded the linen neatly and set it beside the ewer. "Do you prefer balls or soirees?" he asked.

"Balls," she answered. "I enjoy dancing."

"You're quite good at it." He ran a comb through his hair, straightening what he could until Hodges made an appearance to do it for him.

"Almost as good as you are at deflecting questions." She tilted her chin, having clearly made an accurate point. "And almost as good as I am at games. I will be the victor today."

Before he could say anything further, her maid, Edith, entered the room with the tray of hot chocolate, bobbed a quick curtsey, and set about her tasks for the day.

Soon he would see exactly how good Julia was. They both had much to gain. And even more to lose.

CHAPTER 6

That kiss. That kiss, *that kiss*. Julia's insides simply swam at the memory. The very thought conjured a low thrum of anticipation throbbing between her thighs. No matter what she did, she could not clear it from her mind. And if she was being honest, she did not wish to refrain from remembering.

No, she wanted to replay it over and over in her mind. His tongue stroking hers, his teeth nipping at her lower lip. His sensual growl.

A shiver ran down her spine and left her skin prickled with sensual awareness.

"You are cold," Cecelia said from beside her in a soft tone. "Let's have the maid fetch your shawl."

"No need." Julia closed the book on the page she'd attempted to read for the twentieth time. "I'll go upstairs myself. I need to move around a bit, I think." Though really, Julia hoped to find her husband upstairs. As much as she had wanted to avoid him yesterday, she wanted to see him today. After such a kiss, hopefully he could be easily enticed into more.

Cecelia lowered her own book. "I'll come with you."

"I'm perfectly fine." Julia said. "It will only take a moment."

"If you're certain." Cecelia was already settling her gaze on the open novel.

"Very." With that, Julia departed the room, making her way past Nancy's oldest daughter, Lady Penelope, who had an upside-down Gothic novel in her hands and another book resting at its center. One with graphic pages of various plants and...was that an eye?

"Your book is upside down," Julia whispered.

Lady Penelope's mouth dropped open, and the young lady rushed to flip it upright before sliding a sheepishly grateful smile in Julia's direction. That done, Julia dashed up the stairs, a mite too quickly perhaps, in the hopes of seeing William and doing what she could do entice him. Yes, even in the daylight.

A sound came from the other side of her door. Was it rustling? Yes, it was most certainly rustling. Without hesitation, she opened the door, and about gave poor Hodges an apoplexy.

He recovered quickly and bowed. "Your Grace."

She glanced discreetly around their living space to see if William was about. "I came to get my shawl."

"His Grace is not here," he said in a knowing tone.

She regarded the older man as he straightened several bottles of shaving soap and cologne. "I imagine his perpetual neatness makes being his valet easier."

"I much preferred it the other way, Your Grace." Hodges's thin mouth set into a hard line beneath his white mustache.

It was impossible not to notice there was something deeper being alluded to. She ought not to ask. She ought not to care. Even as she reminded herself of these things, her mouth opened up and popped out with a question. "Was he not always so neat?"

Hodges's eyes crinkled with affection. "Oh no, when he was a lad, he was messy as a squirrel."

Julia shook her head at the notion of her immaculate husband being anything but.

She should leave well enough alone and return downstairs. And yet, she yearned to discover what made William strive so terribly hard for perfection. And once more, before she could stop herself from caring, another question emerged. "What changed?"

The light dulled in Hodges's affable expression. "His Grace was changed, that's what. After the fire. I didn't see him again until he took me on as his valet, when he returned home from university. He doesn't speak of his life before then, but I know his relatives shuffled him about for years. I imagine in a situation where one feels like a misstep would mean another house, one learns to be unfailingly perfect."

He lowered his head, revealing a bald spot at the cowlick on the back of his head. "Forgive me, Your Grace. I shouldn't speak so openly. I only wanted you to understand his constant cleaning is by no means an insult to you." His eyes widened. "Not that you're untidy."

She waved her hand dismissively. "Oh, but I am. Terribly messy. Enough for the both of us." The idea of her husband as a young man was a sobering one. Ushered between houses, trying to be perfect, to please them all. "Thank you for telling me."

Hodges held out a pale green shawl for her. It was not the one she would have chosen, but at second glance, it complimented the small embroidery along the hem and was far more becoming than the one Julia had intended. Shawl in hand, she made her way downstairs to find the men had joined the women. The books had all been put away, and Nancy's daughters and Cecelia's younger sister had returned to their private rooms.

Lord Mortry stood in the corner surrounded by every lady in attendance; even Lady Doursly, whose cross face had softened into something almost whimsical as he read aloud from what sounded to be *The Bride of Abydos*. Lord Byron. Of course.

The other gentlemen were gathered around the table with a stack of cards. The other gentlemen, except for William. He sat at a single table near the hearth with an empty seat across from him and a set chess game at the ready.

She approached him with a slow smile. "Is this for us?"

He grinned in reply.

Julia had never been very good at chess, and so her loss came by as no surprise. Unfortunate though it certainly was.

"Checkmate." William leaned forward in his seat with his queen held in his long elegant fingers, and gently tipped over Julia's king with the queen's wide base. He lowered his voice. "Meet me in our chamber."

Before she could even reply, he got to his feet and was gone, leaving her hot and breathless with anticipation. He would no doubt choose a kiss again, but oh how she wanted it. *Needed* it.

She waited a long moment, then slowly, intentionally rose from her chair and slipped out of the room to follow.

WILLIAM COULD SCARCELY WAIT for Julia to arrive. When she did, he caught her by the waist with one arm, and closed the door with the other. He pressed her back gently against the wall, his mouth on hers as her lips parted to accept him.

"What's your prize?" she murmured.

He swept his tongue against hers and cradled her head in his hands, angling her face. "Kissing," he groaned.

A helpless whimper came from the back of her throat. If he wasn't so damn hot and hard, he might have laughed. His plan was working exceedingly well. Even if the act of winning was proving torturous.

Her hands slid across his stomach and down to curl around his solid erection. He grunted in bittersweet surprise. The wonderful, teasing friction, the promise in the cradle of her palm, it was nearly more than he could take.

He removed her hand and pressed his hips to hers, letting her feel all of what she wanted. Her leg shifted up his body, and he knew beneath all those layers, her most intimate place opened with that simple action. Willing and eager to accept him. His breath came ragged, while his hips flexed forward in a motion of lust.

Julia ground her body against his with a desperation he knew all too well. Perhaps it was time to push her farther. Give her more.

He trailed his mouth down the elegant column of her throat as his hand worked free the modest neckline of her frock, taking care to brush her sensitive nipples at all opportunities. Her breasts were lovely. Creamy white and tipped with straining, taut pink buds.

He bent his head and licked the hard nub. Julia's fingers clawed into the back of William's jacket. He then sucked the bud into the heat of his mouth while his tongue stroked gentle circles.

She gasped his name, the sound like sensual honey to his ears. This was suddenly not enough for him either. He wanted to bring her incredible pleasure.

He wanted to consume her thoughts and burn his way into her heart. He wanted to change everything he had done wrong on their wedding night, when his fear of hurting her had stifled him. Now he would ensure all went very, very right.

He straightened and nuzzled her face with his, putting his mouth to her ear. "Are you frustrated, my love?"

"Yes," she whimpered.

"Do you want me?" The question came out on a possessive growl.

Her only reply was a moan, and her weight pressing against him as her knees buckled.

He skimmed his palm down her body to the heat between her legs. "Here?" His middle finger reached out in a languid caress between all those layers of cloth.

She drew in a sharp breath. "Yes. Yes. Yes. *Please* yes."

It was on the edge of his mind to tell her to win the next game, but his mind was hardly working at this point. He lifted her skirts and drew back to watch her expression as he did so.

Those bright blue eyes remained fixed on him, half-lidded and bright with desire. Her mouth was swollen and red from their kisses; her breasts exposed and beautiful. His cock was near bursting just looking at her. Especially when the skirts were properly lifted and pushed over her hips to reveal the thatch of dark hair and an obvious dampness at the apex of her thighs.

Had any woman ever been so wet with need?

He cupped the intimate place. Her brows flinched and the fragile muscles at her neck tensed.

"Here?" he confirmed.

She gave a vigorous nod.

His middle finger moved against her, without the barrier of cloth this time, gliding against what was slick and hot and swollen. "Here?"

She moaned. Her hips bucked against his hand and ground with frustrated intention.

He traced her once, twice, before locating the small bud and rubbing it with the pad of his finger. Her sharp gasp rang out.

"There," she panted. "There."

"Not only there." He slipped a finger inside her where it gripped him with a tightness he remembered too well.

"And there," she agreed in a gasp.

He moved the finger in and out before adding a second. Her hips rocked against his hand in a rhythm that matched his stroking.

"Perhaps both?" He positioned his thumb over the sensitive nub, as his fingers continued to pump inside her.

Julia's eyes flew open. "It's too much."

"It's just enough." He slowed his ministrations. "Trust me, my love."

She nodded, and he kissed her, tasting her lust while he brought her pleasure. She stiffened. Her grip clamping his fingers spasmed and she cried out her euphoria against his mouth. His prick jerked at the sound.

William stroked her only a time or two more before sliding his hand free and releasing her skirts.

She blinked up at him.

"That should have been our wedding night," he said with regret. "I was too afraid of hurting you."

"None of that hurt." She closed her eyes and gave a lazy, languid smile. "I want to do that again."

He wouldn't survive a second time. Even now, his cock ached with indignation. "Oh, we will. Many times."

She chuckled, the sound low and sensual, and he knew well that the decision to give her pleasure had been a good one. His plan was working.

CHAPTER 7

D inner was a far less extravagant affair than the previous days but was by no means without elegance or proper decorum. After all, one did not generally anticipate several extra days in a house party due to a blizzard striking in March.

In truth, Julia could have been served mealworms and probably would not have noticed. Not when her body was still soaring from all those lovely sensations William had wrought upon her simply with the movement of his hand. And now he sat at her side, handsome and charming, engaging in polite conversation as though none of it had happened.

But it had. Oh, it definitely had. The occasional side glance he slid her way told her he was anticipating the next time as much as she was.

But that was not the only thing she continued to remember. Hodges's words prodded at her as well. The reason William was so perfect. He'd had spent the better part of his life making himself immaculate, so he could stay in a home where he was inevitably sent away from regardless. And now, he was once more trying to be perfect to keep her.

The very idea tugged at the inside of her chest.

Her mind twisted, wrestling between the real William she was beginning to discover, and the fear she harbored that he might someday break her heart. What she did know was that the simple act of leaving him, even to use the necessary, made her ache to be with him once more.

That was not a good sign, was it?

After reaching the retiring room and convincing a very naughty Bruiser to wait patiently outside, Julia entered to find Lady Jane dabbing her eyes.

Her bright gaze found Julia's. "Do you think he likes me? Lord Hesterton, I mean."

Julia suppressed a cringe at the question. It was obvious the man was trying to be rid of the failed match attempt. "Why do you ask?"

"The topic of marriage came up at dinner. First Lord Mortry declared he would never trust his heart to a woman. With his terrible past, it's so easy to see why, the poor dear. And then Noah proclaimed he had no wish to marry a pretty young thing who is merely out to get his title and wealth."

"That is why you believe he doesn't like you?" Julia asked.

Lady Jane nodded miserably.

"What do you like about him?" Julia asked.

Lady Jane blinked. "He's a marquis."

"And what else?" Julia prodded. "His pleasant demeanor? His willingness to try new things?" She barely managed not to laugh.

"What did you like about the duke?" Lady Jane asked.

Well, now, that was a good question, wasn't it? Julia had been glad for the opportunity to escape her home. But it had been more than that.

"He was kind." Julia smiled softly at the memories of when they were courting. "He's such a large man, and yet his touch was always gentle, his words always soft spoken and considerate."

Lady Jane furrowed her brow. "I don't think anything about Lord Hesterton is soft..."

"Do you like that?" Julia asked.

The younger woman shook her head.

Lady Doursly shoved into the room, followed by the little white dog that immediately attached himself to Julia's side.

"Jane," Lady Doursly snapped. "Lord Hesterton is outside this very door."

"Mama, I do not believe—"

"This very door," Lady Doursly repeated in a hiss. She grabbed her daughter and pulled her into the hall. Julia followed in time to see Lord Hesterton spin away and quickly limp in the opposite direction. Lady Doursly walked toward him. He moved with more haste. Lady Doursly matched his pace and the hunted marquis limped faster still.

Lady Jane, however, held back. "Thank you for your advice, Your Grace. I found it most enlightening."

"As did I," Julia said to herself. Not that it mattered, for Lady Jane was already making her way back to the salon for the games.

Julia followed slowly, her mind lost in her observation of William. He *was* kind, and always had a way of making her feel safe. Even their lackluster consummation had been the direct result of him not wishing to hurt her. Surely, such a man was trustworthy.

When she entered, the salon's candles were half snuffed out and a large punchbowl had been set at a table's center, which the guests gathered around. The distinct aroma of brandy hung in the air.

"Snapdragon." Nancy clapped her hands. "Who is going first?"

The game had always frightened Julia. The entire bowl was to be lit aflame and people had to pluck a fat raisin from the fiery depths. She had never played the game herself.

"I think the Duke of Stedton ought to take the lead." A dry, papery voice spoke up. Everyone in the room turned to find Lord Venerton, quite awake, his dark eyes glittering in the semi-darkness.

William gave a charming smile and stepped forward. "By all means." He rolled up the sleeve of his left arm, the one without the burn.

A servant touched a candle to the brandy, and blue flames leapt to life over the smooth surface amid the gasps and delighted coos of the small crowd. A muscle worked along William's jaw and the jovial expression on his face looked more carved than natural.

It was cruel to make a man who had narrowly escaped from fire to plunge his good arm into a bowl of it. No doubt Lord Venerton knew as much.

Apparently, he did deserve his wife.

"Come now," Julia said. "Shouldn't it be ladies first?"

William startled and glanced down at her, his bared forearm held aloft. Even Cecelia cast her a curious glance at her sudden interjection.

"I'll have a go of it, if you don't mind, Your Grace." Before her husband could protest, Julia pushed her sleeve's dangling lace from her elbow and plunged her hand into the fire.

The brandy was warm, but even the flames were not hot where they whispered harmlessly over her skin. This was not nearly as frightening as she had always assumed. Her fingers skirted along the bottom, seeking out the lump of an unseen raisin. One brushed at her fingertips.

Blast. She'd missed it.

Her hand pushed forward and nudged the thing again. She

chased it about the bowl, determined not only to catch the confounded thing, but to win the game. After all, when she won, she could choose her own prize.

Her arm was stretched out over the wide bowl now. The raisin couldn't escape her now.

"Your Grace, mind your sleeve," Cecelia said, her voice tight with anxiety.

But the hunt was on. And one deft little grab was all Julia needed to grasp the raisin and win the game. Julia straightened and was met with a flash of light.

"You're on fire," Nancy exclaimed.

Julia jerked back, but the flames came with her. She was truly on fire.

FIRE, an all-consuming beast that destroyed everything in its wake, turning lives to ash. Years had passed, and yet still William could recall the torment of it on his skin, the flames licking over healthy flesh and burning it away.

He had lived in fear of it, never even smoking cheroots or getting too close to a hearth.

Until the moment Julia's arm lit up with those wicked tongues of fire. He acted immediately, tugging his jacket free, wrapping her in it and using his own body to smother the flames.

Everyone stood in a moment of stunned silence before erupting in cheers and gasps of relief. He hardly heard them. He instead stared at the blossoming spots of red on Julia's arm amid the singed lace. "You're hurt."

Lady Cecelia was at his wife's side in a blink, eyes wide with concern. "You've been burned."

"Only a little." Julia fingered the blackened edge of lace. "My gown is certainly ruined."

"Oh, Julia, I'm terribly sorry." Lady Bursbury rushed forward and pushed a wad of linen into William's hand.

It was cold against his palm, the cloth filled with snow to act as a cooling compress. "I'll see to her upstairs."

Lady Bursbury blinked rapidly and dabbed at her glossy eyes. "Yes, of course," she choked. "Please do let us know if you need anything."

Bursbury was at his wife's side at the show of distress, his arm around her. "Perhaps we should resume games tomorrow." He snapped his fingers. "Bruiser, out."

The white fluff of a dog slunk away from the table of abandoned raisins.

"Naughty thing." Julia gave a good-natured chuckle. A solid sign she was not severely injured.

"He must be used to someone feeding him the food meant for his betters," William muttered and slid Julia a side glance. "Let's get you seen to."

In the few moments it took to arrive at their chambers, the Bursbury staff had already delivered a healing salve and fresh linen for binding. Hodges remained as the only servant in the room.

"Edith cannot tolerate the sight of injuries," Julia said by way of explanation.

"How terribly inconvenient." He extended her arm. "Let me see."

Julia obeyed, shifting her elbow to display the burn. "I don't get injured often."

William nodded to Hodges, silently conveying he would see to Julia and the servant was dismissed. Hodges slipped from the room, while William studied the splotches of red on his wife's forearm.

"Was it the fire?" Julia asked.

"I'm certain this did not come from feeding Bruiser under the table." He lifted his gaze from her injury to meet her wide blue eyes.

"Not my arm," she said softly. "Your parents."

And just like that, with the simple reminder, the wound in his chest ripped open anew. "Yes." He plucked the stopper from the salve.

"What happened?" she asked, her tone the vocal equivalent of a tiptoe.

I killed them. With my indecision and hesitation. I lived, and they died.

"I don't talk about it." He dipped his fingers in the greasy salve. "This may hurt."

He was exceedingly careful when spreading the balm over her arm, almost not touching her at all. He remembered far too well how the slightest of brushes on charred skin brought pain. Her injury was not as bad as his had been, but he would not take any chances.

She did not flinch, not from the touch, nor from his refusal to answer. "Who did you live with after the fire?"

Her words prodded at his wounds, even as he so gently administered a balm to hers. "My aunt."

"Until your maturity?"

"No."

She bit her bottom lip and watched him with a quiet intensity. "How old were you when it happened?"

He put the top back on the jar of balm and wiped his hands clean on an extra square of linen. "Seven."

She gave a soft cry. He jerked his attention back to her, thinking she'd injured the burned part of her arm. Instead, he found her staring at him in horror.

"Only seven?" Her fingertips went to her lips. "You were just a boy."

He brushed off her concern. "It didn't exactly happen last year. At any rate, it's old news that no one need talk about any longer." He lifted up the gauzy white bandage the Bursbury's had provided.

She cradled her arm to her chest, keeping it from him. "Frustrated or angry?"

He studied her. "I beg your pardon?"

"Are you frustrated with me for asking these questions?" She tilted her head in genuine curiosity. "Or are you angry?"

"It isn't my topic of choice, but I'm not angry with you." He ran a hand over his jaw and paused, possibly detecting a rough patch. A second pass over the area reassured him there was indeed not a section of his face missed in his last shave. "I'm not frustrated with you, either."

She held her arm out to him to wrap. "I believe it is well within my right to declare myself the winner of snapdragon."

He eyed her arm. Balm glistened over the tender skin. "Are you so sure?"

"Yes." She unfurled her fist to reveal a fat, brandy-soaked raisin at the center of her palm. "And since I am the winner, I have a prize to claim."

Oh, yes. He slowly, tenderly eased the linen over her skin and tried to ignore how his body went instantly hot at the idea of what she wanted. She had made it clear from the beginning what she would request. And while he had been reluctant at first, his own damnable teasing had stretched his control to the limit and made him nearly shake with the idea of touching her. Loving her.

"Yes, you do have a prize to claim." He tucked the edge of her binding against her upper arm where the skin was uninjured. He leaned toward her and framed her lovely jaw with his fingertips, his mouth easing closer to hers. "Dare I ask what you'll request?"

"I want..." Her brow furrowed slightly, and she studied him for a long moment, casting her gaze from his eyes to his lips and back again. "I want..."

She was having a hard time saying it, but he would not have a hard time giving it. He waited patiently, knowing exactly what she would say.

He couldn't have been more wrong.

CHAPTER 8

J ulia knew what she ought to ask for. It was what she'd been after since the beginning.

And yet, things had changed.

Her prior curiosity that had spurred her conversation with Hodges now tipped to concern. She desired William, yes. Especially after what he'd done to her body only hours before. Especially when his mouth hovered so close to her own, the spicy scent of him making her arc toward him with yearning.

But there was so much more. She needed to know not just the man, but also the boy who had made this man who he was.

It was her solitary win and she knew exactly what she would ask for.

She lifted her hand to his face, where the grain of his whiskered jaw had been meticulously scraped to softness. "I want to know about your childhood, about your parents, about the fire, and Maribel."

He blinked. "I'm sorry?"

"Forgive me, I know you thought that I would request, you know." A blush flared over her cheeks. "But I would like to know what happened. It's part of discovering you, William, and to do that I need to truly understand you."

He leaned back, putting a more breathable, less heart-catching distance between them. He cleared his throat, then rattled his history off with a swift, detached efficiency. "The country estate caught on fire when I was a boy. My parents died because of me. I would have perished too, were it not for Hodges. I was passed around from house to house because no one wants an orphan. Maribel was my father's favorite horse. She's very sick and will soon die."

The casual lift of his shoulders indicated the end.

But even in that brief tale, there was so, so much.

"Because of you?" Julia repeated. "How could you have possibly caused your parents' deaths?"

He stared down at his hands. "I was in the study, where I wasn't supposed to be. I knew there was a fire and I froze." He rubbed his fingers together, and then balled his hand in a fist. "I was so afraid I would get in trouble for being in the study that I remained there too long trying to decide what best to do to get out of the situation. My parents were calling me and when I finally emerged, they were on the other side of the split-level stairs. Their side collapsed. The one I was on began to sway and Hodges grabbed me. When I awoke, I'd lost my parents. My family."

Julia's heart contracted for the boy who spent a lifetime thinking his parents' deaths were his fault. She reached out and took his hands in hers. "It wasn't your fault."

"I don't know that I'll ever believe that." He lowered his head. "My guilt made me a terror. I misbehaved badly and was sent from the first three homes before I realized I needed to improve my behavior. The better I was, the more invisible I became, the longer I lasted. I stayed with my father's cousin for two years, though most of that time I was away at school."

"That's why you try so hard to be perfect," Julia surmised.

He lifted his head and gave a mirthless smile.

And now he was being perfect to keep her. She flinched at the painful realization.

"What do you want?" she asked through numb lips. "More than anything?"

His eyes met hers, deep brown and sincere. "A family."

Julia could almost hear the crack as her heart broke for him, for the family he'd lost and the family she had been fighting to keep from him.

His hands tightened on hers. "Please give me a chance, Julia."

A log settled in the hearth, and something deep within the glowing center popped and hissed. William tensed.

"You're afraid of fire, aren't you?" she asked.

He lifted a brow.

"I saw you hesitate," she explained. "At the brandy bowl."

"And you saved me," he said apologetically.

"You were the one who saved me. Even though I was surrounded in the one thing you feared most. Why?"

He pulled his hands free from hers and cupped her face in his palms. "Because I love you, Julia. I've loved you since the day I asked Lady Bursbury for an introduction and she got it in her head to play matchmaker. I saw how your eyes lingered on me at the first ball we attended together, and I couldn't get you out of my mind. It's why I asked to court you immediately, why I married you so quickly." His thumb brushed her cheek. "I love you enough to let you go, if that is truly what you wish." He pressed a kiss to her brow and settled his forehead against hers. "But it is not what I want."

"William." His name emerged from her tight throat in a catch.

He pressed his thumb to her mouth, sealing it. "Don't say

anything, please. I just want you to understand what you mean to me."

With that, he got to his feet.

Julia snapped her head up. "Where are you going?"

"To let Lady Bursbury know you are well. She's terribly worried." He swept a hand over Julia's hair in an affectionate caress. "And to allow you time to think over what I've said."

But she didn't have to think. She already knew. This man who had faced his fears to save her, who had lost everything and sought only to gain back the wholeness of his heart, she had to give him a chance. She had to give *herself* a chance.

He paused at the door. "To be fair, I do not count this as your prize. If you would like to claim another, I will offer no complaints." Then he was gone.

She couldn't help the smile on her lips any more than she could dim the lightness in her soul. For she knew her fears about William were unfounded.

That was not all she had reconciled within her soul. She was finally ready to admit what she had felt the first time those warm brown eyes met hers. It had fueled her suspicion and put a visceral edge to her fear, and now she finally understood why: she loved her husband.

She always had.

WILLIAM HAD SPENT most of his life behind a shield, steeling himself and his heart from rejection. However, the baring of his deepest hurt and greatest wish to Julia did not leave him as achingly vulnerable as he had anticipated. No, he felt comforted, the rocky bed of his childhood finally smoothed.

She knew now what he wanted, and why he wanted it. He

only hoped it would be enough to change her mind. Not that he would ever stop trying if it didn't.

Lady Bursbury had been exceedingly grateful he had informed her Julia's burn was minor and she would recover easily. He'd never seen Lady Bursbury in such a nervous state, and she'd continued to apologize profusely, despite it not being any real fault of hers.

As he approached the chamber to return to Julia, the door to his right opened and Lady Venerton stepped out. She caught his gaze and her eyes widened. "Your Grace," she gasped.

Quickly, she shut her door and swept toward him.

William stiffened and resisted the very rude urge to take a step away from her. The odor of brandy hovered around her like a fog.

"I wanted to talk to you," she said in a breathy whisper.

William exhaled to avoid being victim to her pungent breath. Good God, had the woman drank a full decanter on her own?

"Lady Venerton, my wife has been injured, if you'll recall—"

"That is what I wanted to talk to you about." Lady Venerton pushed her shoulders back so her small breasts were shoved high on her chest. She lowered her head in a way she must have intended to be seductive, except it made her look as fully foxed as she smelled, eyes half-mast and mouth slack. "She doesn't deserve you. I know men like you. Strong, healthy, virile. You need—"

"This is highly inappropriate." William turned from the woman.

She grabbed his arm, her grip strong. Before he could realize what the countess was doing, she threw her body against him. William flew back against the wall at the unexpected press of weight and knocked a vase from the table. It crashed to the floor, and Lady Venerton's mouth pressed wetly against his.

A soft cry came from somewhere behind Lady Venerton.

"William."

He recognized that voice. Oh God, he recognized that voice.

Julia.

CHAPTER 9

J ulia couldn't think. She could only run. Away from the scene, away from the hurt. Away from the husband who had betrayed her.

"Julia—wait." William shouted somewhere behind her, but she didn't stop. Not even when the aged Lord Venerton ran past her, nearly knocking her to the ground.

"I knew there was something between the two of you," a reedy voice hissed.

Julia turned in time to see him deliver a solid blow to William. She was not the only victim.

Her heart clattered in her chest. Heat blazed through her and made the pain in her arm agonizing. The warmth seemed to press into her lungs and fog her brain. She needed to get outside. Just for a moment. Just to breathe.

She raced through the front door and slammed directly into a person. She reeled back and looked up to find Lord Hesterton staring down at her as though she'd grown a second head.

"It's cold out here, Your Grace." His obvious statement was delivered with his usual bored drawl.

The chill in the air washed over her like a cool cloth. "I need to get some air," she gasped. "To just...forgive me, but to just be alone."

"Now that I understand." He gave her a soft smile. "Will you at least accept my coat?"

Was she not wearing a coat? Her mind spun. Of course, she wasn't. She hadn't time to put one on.

She nodded, and he pulled the coat from his shoulders and draped it over hers. The lining inside was still warm from the heat of his body.

"Thank you," she said in puff of frozen air and rushed from the house.

He called after her, something she could scarcely make out. But she didn't ask him to repeat it. She didn't care. All that mattered was the agonizing chasm filling her chest.

William.

He had betrayed her exactly as her father had done to her mother. She was grateful it had not gone too far. She had not told him she loved him. What a fool she would have been then.

The moon cast its brilliant light overhead and turned the world into a wash of purple blue snow. The wind had stopped, and the night was still.

Lady Venerton.

Louisa.

The vilest of all women.

Julia stiffened.

The vilest of all women.

A woman who easily took what she wanted, even when it was obvious the feelings were not mutual. Julia exclaimed her own stupidity into the night air. She had fallen too quickly on her fears rather than her trust.

She needed to go to William, to get the entire story from him. To know for certain.

A deep, terrible groan came from beneath her feet. Confusion caught her for only a moment and then the terrifying understanding dawned. She had wandered onto the frozen lake.

She spun around to turn in the other direction, when the ice beneath groaned again, and gave a splintering crack.

WILLIAM HELD Lord Venerton's wiry frame back with one arm. The elderly man swung feebly at William, each blow too far away to land.

"I have never had anything to do with your wife, Venerton," William growled. "See to your wife and leave me be."

Lord Venerton regarded his wife.

"I've never struck a woman." William glared at Lady Venerton, who staggered drunkenly and regarded them both with a smug, bleary smile. "And I won't start today," William continued. "But I've never been more tempted."

With that, he raced down the stairs where Julia had gone. Was she in the library? The drawing room perhaps?

Hesterton waved at him. "I believe your wife has lost her mind."

William grabbed the marquis by the shoulders. "Where is she?"

"Outside, wandering about on the frozen lake." Hesterton frowned. "I tried to tell her—"

Whatever the man said, William didn't hear. He was already flying out the door to find Julia. The icy air slammed into him and seared his lungs. He searched the moonlit snow until he settled on a figure in the distance. Directly on the lake.

He ran to her, faster than he'd ever run before, and bellowed her name. The figure didn't move.

"William, don't come here." A note pitched Julia's voice and tugged at his heart.

She didn't want to see him. But he didn't give a damn. First, he would get her off the ice, then he would demand she listen, then—

A crack shattered the silence followed by a startled scream.

William did not hesitate. Not like he had when the house had caught fire and his parents had died. No, this time he lurched forward.

He lowered himself to his chest on the snow-covered ice and called for her to do the same. Another crack came at the same time he spoke, this one longer and louder than before. The sound increased with such ferocity, his head snapped up. No sooner had he done so, Julia fell through the ice with a splash, her scream cut short.

William shoved forward so hard, he glided over the ice to where the hole showed like ink against the white of the snow. Her slender arms gripped the jagged edge. He grabbed her forearms and yanked up with all the strength he'd ever possessed. She flew out of the water and landed at his side, sputtering and blinking.

The ice splintered around them.

"Keep on your stomach and scoot." He held her hand tightly in his.

She did as he instructed, her movements stiff and jerking. They edged away from the broken ice, but still he did not relax.

Julia slowed, and the puffs of her breath came heavier. She was tiring. William held her hand tighter and pulled her with him in an attempt to ease her efforts.

"I didn't do it," he gritted from between his teeth.

"I know." Her voice was weak.

She was fading. He could lose her still. The shore was still a fair distance away. He gripped her to his side, holding her in his arms as he dragged them both.

"We're nearly there," he said by way of encouragement.

The ice snapped somewhere in the distance, a savage beast nipping at their heels. By God, he would get them out of this.

"I'm sorry." Julia gave a violent shiver. "I shouldn't have run off."

They reached the shore. Finally.

He leapt to his feet and lifted her into his arms. Even drenched with icy water, her weight was easily borne. Carrying her, he made quick work of the walk to the house and met with the very concerned crowd of party guests, most especially Lady Cecelia and Lady Bursbury. The latter of whom waved her fingers toward the lot of them, shooing them about like small children until a path formed.

"Is she dead?" Lord Mortry peered curiously at her, as William passed.

William glared at him. "No."

Lady Bursbury ignored Lord Mortry and rushed along beside William. "The servants had water already heated for a bath for Lady Venerton. I've instructed them instead to move it to your room. It will be at the ready for you."

William nodded his thanks.

Lady Bursbury pressed a hand to her chest. "Mercy me, this has been a night!"

Indeed, it had, but William didn't waste time on those words. Not when his only concern was getting Julia upstairs and warmed in that bath.

CHAPTER 10

J ulia had never been so cold in her entire life. She could barely think for the shivers rattling through her. William's strong arms kept her pressed against him, no matter how violently she shuddered, up the stairs, through the door, and into the privacy of their chamber.

"I know you're cold, my love." He lowered her to her feet before a bath tub. "We need to get you out of this gown and into the water."

She hugged herself in an effort to trap in some heat. "I c...can't—"

"I'll do it."

She faced the steaming water, while he worked over the fastenings. At one point, a quiet rending interrupted the pop, pop, popping of the line of buttons. She didn't care. All she wanted was heat. The gown fell heavily from her body and slapped in a wet pile to the floor. Her corset followed, then her shift. Next was her stockings, and she was left completely naked and shivering in front of him.

Ordinarily, she would have been embarrassed, but there was no thought of that. Not now. Not until she was submerged in the heat of the water and the initial pain faded to the prickling tingles of heat that warmed her body to something languid.

"Do you want some tea?" William asked once she'd stopped shivering.

"In the bath?" She couldn't help but chuckle.

"Are you still cold?" He frowned and put a hand into the water. Ripples arced away from his hand and lapped over her skin.

"It's wonderfully hot."

Noting the relaxed tone to her voice, he shifted his focus to her face, his brow still furrowed. "Lady Venerton threw herself at me. Quite literally."

"I belatedly realized as much. I only reacted as I did because of my father, because of what he did to my mother." Julia sighed, and the swell of her breasts rose slightly from the water.

William's gaze slipped to the rise of her bosom for one pulse-stopping moment before returning to her face. "I'm devoted to you, Julia. When we were courting, and now, and on through forever. I want you and only you."

"You want me?" She sighed again, long and purposeful.

His gaze lowered once more, and he swallowed. "There's nothing I want more in my life."

"I believe you said I'm owed a prize still." She shifted in the tub to arch her back. "Is that correct?"

He nodded.

The swish of water against her skin went from soothing to sensual, each sway and brush against her skin made her body hum with pleasure.

"In the bed?" She tilted her head in a wicked grin. "Or in the tub?"

He hesitated. "Are you sure? This night has not been kind to you."

"Then make it so and answer the question." She slipped a

wet, naked leg from the water and let it dangle over the edge in front of him.

His stare followed the action. "Definitely in the tub."

"Not with your clothes on," she chided.

If he'd removed her attire with haste, he did so doubly fast with his own until he stood before her, chiseled with muscle and wonderfully nude. The firelight flickered golden shadows over his beautiful body. He was perfect. Even the scars crisscrossing jagged lines over his arm made him even more so, a symbol of his survival, of what he'd lived through and overcome. Julia's gaze trailed down the expanse of his chest and lower still to where the hard maleness of him jutted in anticipation.

"I won't hurt you," he promised.

"Don't be too careful, either." She curled her finger to beckon him closer.

He obeyed, stepping carefully into the tub and sinking into the fragranced bath with her. Waves slapped against the side of the copper tub, but she scarcely noticed. Their knees were pushed against one another, everything touching in the snug confines of the otherwise large tub.

She sat up as he leaned forward, their mouths coming together in hungry, panting breaths, their bodies slick and hot pressing to one another.

The light sprinkling of hair on his chest and legs crinkled against her skin, sending lovely ripples of pleasure through her.

"You're so beautiful, Julia." He trailed kisses down her chest.

She pushed her bosom toward him, hungry for the heat of his mouth on her again. He suckled first one nipple, then the other, his tongue flicking teasing circles against the little nubs. Her hands moved beneath the water, seeking and ultimately finding, the hard staff of his desire.

He grunted against her breast.

She froze. "Does that hurt?"

"Only as much as this." His hand slid up her inner thigh to cup the apex of her thighs. A finger slid up her center, gliding with the most delicious friction.

She gripped him more firmly and slid her hand from length to tip. She explored him thus as his fingers deftly brought her to the brink.

"Not yet." He dragged his mouth from her breasts to her neck, kissing, nipping. His breath rasped in her ear, his voice silky when he spoke. "Part your legs for me."

His arm slipped behind her shoulder blades, softening the hard edge of the tub. She did as he bade, spreading her knees to accommodate the weight of him between her thighs. The tip of his staff bobbed clumsily at that intimate place.

With one hand in the water, he watched her carefully with eyes so dark they appeared black. The clumsy bumps ceased and something firm pressed at her entrance. She gasped in delight.

The banded muscles of his stomach clenched, and he slowly flexed his hips forward. His length eased into her, only an inch or so. But it was enough to make her want more. She whimpered in frustration and lifted her hips higher to meet him.

He took her mouth in a kiss where teeth scraped lips and tongues stroked with abandon. The gentle push inside her worked into small thrusts, each one sinking deeper than the last. Waves undulated the water, lapping and sloshing as he filled her one careful inch at a time.

She locked her legs around him, holding him to her. He drew out and back in, pumping pleasure through her while she rocked against him to catch every sensation. His hand moved between her thighs to stroke the bud of her sex. Her body tensed, knowing what was coming, and welcoming it.

"I love you," she panted. "I love you, I love you, I love you." On the last phrase, the exhilaration overwhelmed her. She flew over the edge of her climax as William's thrusts shortened into hard, fast jerks.

He buried his face against her neck and groaned. The fullness inside of her pulsed and she knew she had what she wanted. Only this time, she did not wish for a child so she could have a life on her own. She wished for a child to begin the family they would build together.

WILLIAM CRADLED JULIA AGAINST HIM. Long after the bath had been cleared away, and the house had gone quiet with sleep, they had lain awake together. Sometimes touching, sometimes talking, learning one another in every wonderful way imaginable.

"Country estate, or London?" he asked in her ear.

"Wherever I'm with you." Her voice was slurred with the need to sleep.

"I like that answer." And he did. She had faced her own fear and pushed through it to trust him. It was a tender, fragile thing he held in the cradle of his heart. One he would never break.

Her cheek moved against his and he knew she was smiling.

He pressed a kiss to the shallow dip just below her ear. "Thank you."

"Hmmm?" she hummed in a lazy tone, clearly somewhere between sleep and wakefulness.

"For giving me your trust."

She rolled over and lazily regarded him with tender affection. "And thank you."

He lifted his brow for her to go on.

She chuckled. "For teaching me to love so beautifully." Her wink was coquettish. "For saving me. Twice." She stroked a hand over his jaw. "For letting me discover you."

"My love." He pulled her into his arms and lay her head on his chest. "It has been my pleasure."

EPILOGUE
LONDON, MAY 1816

J ulia opened the small card with anticipation. Lady
Bursbury's notes always included welcome news and invita-
tions. This one was no exception.

"We've been invited to attend a musical featuring Lady Penelope," Julia said to William as she scanned the neat script. "I
cannot believe she's come out already. It makes me feel positively ancient."

William peered at her from the edge of his paper. "You're far
from ancient, darling."

She smiled at him. He was always ready to compliment her,
even when two years had passed without her producing any
children. "And Lady Jane is getting married."

William scoffed. "Poor Hesterton."

"No, to Lord Mortry," Julia corrected.

"Then poor Lady Jane."

"Hesterton hasn't been excluded, it appears." Julia read on.
"Nancy is attempting to set up a match between Noah and the
Craig heiress, Miss Helen." She set the invitation on the table
with a flick of delight. Helen was a dear friend of hers through
Cecelia, a woman who was almost as much a social recluse as

their other friend, Emma Thorne, both of whom avoided the ton as much as was possible.

The paper did not move a single crinkle. "It would take an extraordinary woman to edge her way into Hesterton's heart. If he has one."

"Oh, come now," Julia said. "Everyone has a heart, and there's one perfect person for the edging. I think he and Helen would make a delightful couple, especially if Nancy thinks they would get on well."

William turned the page.

The invitation was not the only thing that made Julia's stomach flutter with excitement. She bit back a grin. "Kittens or puppies?"

"Puppies." Another page turn.

"Kittens have their own qualities: slender little tails that jut out like shaky sticks, squeaking mewls, tiny paws. Are you certain?"

"Puppies. Always."

Her heart tripped over itself. "Boys or girls?"

"For puppies or kittens?"

"Neither." A smile curled at her lips as she spoke. "Children."

Whump! Hands and paper dropped at once to the table. William regarded her with tentative excitement, his brows poised halfway up his forehead. "Dare I ask what could inspire such a question?"

She rose from her seat and let her fingers tenderly stroke her lower midsection. "I'm sure you can guess."

"I want to hear you say it."

"Our family will be growing by one more in the next few months." The emotion bubbled up from Julia, and she laughed at the sheer joy of sharing such news. "We're going to be parents, William."

"Are you certain?"

"I waited two months after I missed my courses to be certain." She stopped beside him.

His gaze fell to her stomach. "The physician never came."

"He did." She moved her hand, took his, and placed it over the very small bump. "I waited until you would be out. I didn't wish to worry you, and I didn't want to tell you until I knew for certain."

"You clever minx." He cupped his large hand over her stomach. His brow furrowed, and he was silent for an extraordinarily long moment.

A trickle of fear nipped at her enjoyment. "Happy? Or displeased?"

"Happy." He looked up at her with a glossy gaze. "Immeasurably happy."

This small baby within her womb had moved her brave and powerful husband to tears. She felt her own eyes prickle with heat.

"I love you, Julia." He got to his feet and pulled her into his arms. Immediately he snapped back and regarded her stomach.

She laughed through her tears. "You won't hurt him."

He drew Julia against him once more, this time tender and tentative. "Or her."

"Oh? Is it a girl you want, then?" Julia snuggled into her husband's strong arms.

He held her to him and cupped the slight swell of her stomach once more, cradling his entire family in one embrace. "That depends."

"On?"

"On what this baby is."

"I think that's the perfect answer."

And it was. The perfect answer, for the perfect life and the perfectly wonderful husband she was grateful to have taken the time to discover.

ALSO BY MADELINE MARTIN

The Borderland Ladies

Ena's Surrender

Marin's Promise

Anice's Bargain

Ella's Desire

Catriona's Secret

Leila's Legacy

The Borderland Rebels

The Highlander's Lady Knight

Faye's Sacrifice

Kinsey's Defiance

Clara's Vow

Drake's Honor

Highland Passions

A Ghostly Tale of Forbidden Love

The Madam's Highlander

Her Highland Destiny

The Highlander's Untamed Lady

Matchmaker of Mayfair

Discovering the Duke

Unmasking the Earl

Mesmerizing the Marquis

Earl of Benton

Earl of Oakhurst

Earl of Kendal

Heart of the Highlands

Deception of a Highlander

Possession of a Highlander

Enchantment of a Highlander

Standalones

The Highlander's Challenge - N W M S

Her Highland Beast - N W M S (fairytale twist retelling - Beauty and the Beast/Princess and the Pea with Scottish folklore)

ABOUT THE AUTHOR

Madeline Martin is a *New York Times, USA Today,* and International Bestselling author of historical fiction and historical romance with books that have been translated into over twenty different languages.

She lives in sunny Florida with her two daughters (known collectively as the minions), two incredibly spoiled cats and a man so wonderful he's been dubbed Mr. Awesome. She is a diehard history lover who will happily lose herself in research any day. When she's not writing, researching or 'moming', you can find her spending time with her family at Disney or sneaking a couple spoonfuls of Nutella while laughing over cat videos. She also loves research and travel, attributing her fascination with history to having spent most of her childhood as an Army brat in Germany.

Check out her website for book club visits, reader guides for her historical fiction, upcoming events, book news and more: https://madelinemartin.com

Printed in Great Britain
by Amazon

24688418R00050